THIS MAGI BOOK BELONGS TO:

_____

_____

_____

_____

For Simon, Alison and Laura
– A.H.B.

For Maxim and Olivia
– E.H.

Reprinted 1998 (Twice)

This paperback edition published 1998

First published 1998 by Magi Publications
22 Manchester Street, London W1M 5PG

Text © 1998 A.H.Benjamin
Illustrations © 1998 Elisabeth Holstien

Printed in Belgium by Proost NV, Turnhout

ISBN 1 85430 459 3

A DUCK SO SMALL

by A. H. Benjamin

illustrated by Elisabeth Holstien

Duffle was a very small duck and,
because of his size, all the other ducks
laughed at him.

"A duck so small can do nothing at all!"
they jeered.
"I may be small," thought Duffle sadly,
"but there must be *something* I can do."
He wondered what it could be.

Duffle looked round and noticed
Kingfisher perching on a reed.
He was just about to say hello,
when . . .

. . . Kingfisher suddenly took off and dived,
straight as an arrow, into the water.
"Kingfisher is small," said Duffle, "but see how
    well he dives. Perhaps I could do that, too."

. . . and came down again
like a dropped stone.

"Look what I can do!" Duffle
called out to the other ducks.
He flew high into the air . . .

Duffle hit the water so hard that he nearly bounced off it!

"Ha, ha, ha, what did we say," cried the other ducks. "A duck so small can do nothing at all!"

Poor Duffle felt very foolish.
He climbed out on to the
riverbank, wondering
what to do next.

Duffle saw Heron, standing perfectly still on one leg in the shallow water.

"What good balance she has," thought Duffle. "Perhaps I could do that, too."

"Look what I can do!" Duffle called, as he stood on one leg, with his wings spread out.

He wobbled this way and that and . . .

. . . landed flat on his beak.
"Ha, ha, ha, what did we say," laughed the other
ducks. "A duck so small can do nothing at all!"

Duffle crept off into the shade of a tree so that
the other ducks wouldn't notice his blushes.
Tap, tap, tap, went a sound above his head.

Looking up, Duffle saw Woodpecker making
a hole in the trunk.
"What a strong beak he has," thought the
little duck. "Perhaps I could bore a hole, too."

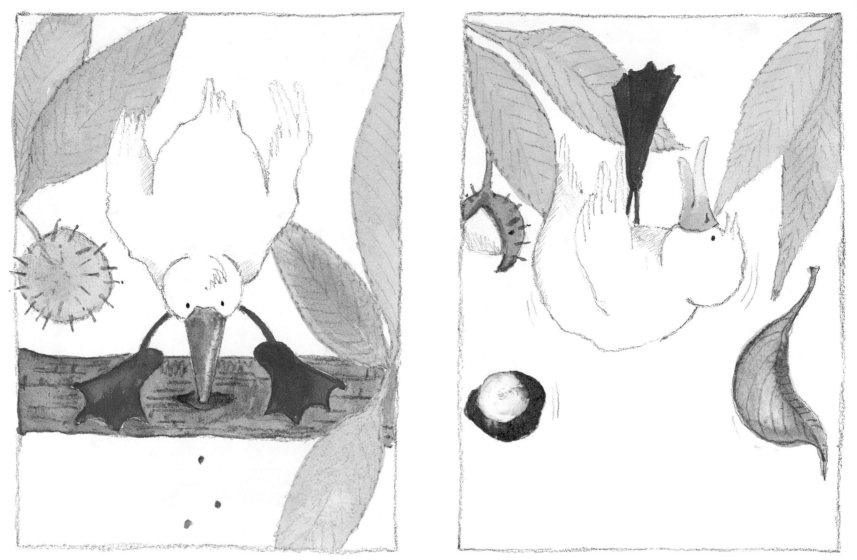

"Look what I can do!" Duffle called out to the other ducks. He flew up into the tree and perched on a thick branch. Peck, peck, peck, he went at the wood. "Oops," he cried, as he lost his balance. Duffle toppled off the branch and . . .

. . . fell to the ground.

"Ha, ha, ha, what did we say," cackled the other
ducks. "A duck so small can do nothing at all!"

All the ducks were paddling and splashing in the river, but poor Duffle decided to hide in the rushes until they left. That way he wouldn't have to listen to their sniggering.

"I'm good at nothing," he thought. "I'm just a small, useless duck." And a tear rolled down his beak.

For a long time, Duffle could still hear those ducks quacking with laughter. It seemed as though they would never leave. "I'll stay here just a bit longer till they get tired of it," he thought. But as he listened, he realised something.

The ducks weren't laughing at him.
They were quacking in alarm!

Duffle paddled over to see what all the fuss was about. It seemed that a duckling had got stuck in a tiny hole in the riverbank.

"Oh, please get him out," begged the duckling's mother.

"We will," said the other ducks, but it was no good.
They were just too big to squeeze into the hole.

All except for Duffle.

"Let *me* try," he said and, because
he was so small, he was able to reach
right in.

It didn't take him long to rescue the trapped duckling.

"Good old Duffle!" cried one duck.
"None of us could have done that," said another.
"A duck so small *can* be useful after all!" quacked a third.

"Oh, it was nothing," blushed Duffle.
And, though he was only a little duck,
he felt bigger and stronger than them all.

Some more books from
Magi Publications
for you to enjoy.

Look Out for the Big Bad Fish!
Sheridan Cain
Tanya Linch

MARK EZRA
The Prickly Hedgehog
Pictures by GAVIN ROWE

TOM'S TAIL
Linda Jennings ◆ Tim Warnes

DORA'S EGGS
by Julie Sykes   Pictures by Jane Chapman

LAZY OZZIE
Michael Coleman
Gwyneth Williamson

Alan MacDonald
BEWARE of the BEARS!
Gwyneth Williamson

All books available from most booksellers. In case of difficulty please contact
Magi Publications, 22 Manchester Street, London W1M 5PG, UK